GREG the SAUSAGE ROLL

To Phoenix and Kobe, never give up on your dreams.

Love Mum and Dad xx - R. H. and M. H.

For Mum & Dad – sausage rolls aren't just for Christmas! (eh, Dad?)

Thank you for all your love and support. - G.C.

PUFFIN BOOKS

UK | USA | Canada | Ireland | Australia | India | New Zealand | South Africa

Puffin Books is part of the Penguin Random House group of companies whose addresses can be found at global.penguinrandomhouse.com

www.penguin.co.uk www.puffin.co.uk www.ladybird.co.uk

First published 2023

001

Illustrations by Gareth Conway

Printed and bound in Italy

The authorized representative in the EEA is Penguin Random House Ireland, Morrison Chambers, 32 Nassau Street, Dublin D02 YH68

A CIP catalogue record for this book is available from the British Library

ISBN: 978-0-241-63109-6

All correspondence to: Puffin Books, Penguin Random House Children's, One Embassy Gardens, 8 Viaduct Gardens, London SW11 7BW

GREG the SAUSAGE ROLL

WISH YOU WERE HERE

MARK AND ROXANNE HOYLE

Illustrated by Gareth Conway

PUFFIN

It was a baking hot summer's day, and everyone at the bakery felt hotter than the hottest hot dog with extra-hot chilli sauce on top!

"I'm MELTING, Gloria!" wailed Greg. "I'm absolutely roasting toasting!"

"Oh Greg," laughed the mini sausage rolls, as flakes of pastry flew over the counter top. "Maybe you could let a few of us share the fan too?"

"But I'm SO HOT!" Greg moaned.
"I wish it was Christmas so we could play in the snow!"

"You ALWAYS wish it was Christmas, Greg!"
exclaimed Gloria.

"I just wish we could all go on holiday – chill on a beach and relax by the pool. Bliss," she sighed.

Just then, a very flustered family burst through the door, chattering excitedly. "Hiya, Holly!" said Mum, as her two boys raced around and around in circles.

"You mean *Hola!*" grinned Dad. "We're off on holiday, Holly, but first I need my sausage roll for the plane, please – I can't last a whole week without one!"

"Coming right up," said Holly, as she picked up her tongs and chose . . .
GREG!

"YES, MATE! I'm going on holidaaaayyyy!" cheered Greg.

"Have the time of your life!" called Gloria.

Greg couldn't BELIEVE how exciting the airport was! He just couldn't wait a second longer.

He leapt out of Dad's backpack and ran as fast as his little legs could carry him. "I'm off to catch a plane!" he cried.

Greg raced through the airport and came to a skidding halt in front of some big departure boards. How could he possibly choose where to go?!

Just then, Greg felt a
WHOOOOOOSH
as two wheelie cases
whirled past him.

"Ooh – they look like they know where they're going!" Greg grabbed a luggage label and clung on tight – he was off to sunny Spain!

Before he knew it, Greg was on an AEROPLANE!
There was so much to explore – in the cockpit, Greg wanted to push ALL the buttons. Luckily, he couldn't *quite* reach them . . .

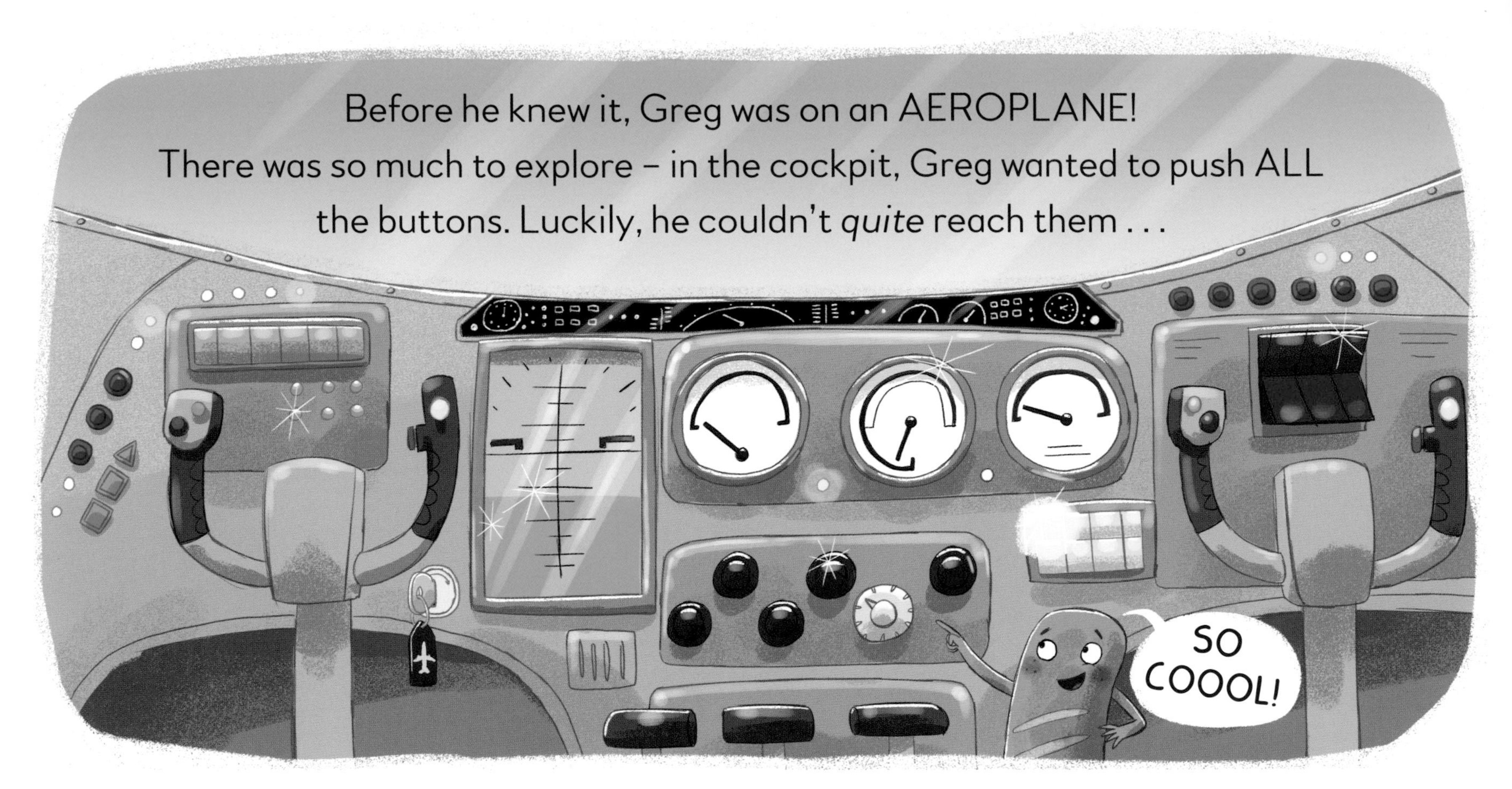

Then Greg hitched a ride on the food trolley.
It was filled with so many tasty treats!

Greg wanted to make some new friends, but everyone seemed VERY busy.

After so much fun exploring, Greg was pooped!
It wasn't long before he started to nod off . . .

When Greg woke up, the plane was empty!
He jumped off his seat and gazed around in alarm.
"Oh no!" he cried. "I hope I haven't missed my holiday!"

"Look everyone – we have a newbie!"
shouted a voice from behind him.

"Where's everybody gone?" asked Greg.

"They've gone on holiday!" replied a kind-looking
chocolate bar. "If you want to go too, you'd better be quick!"

Greg was just in time to catch a ride.

At the terminal, he spotted the suitcase of his dreams . . .
"Take me to Paradise!" beamed Greg as he shimmied in.

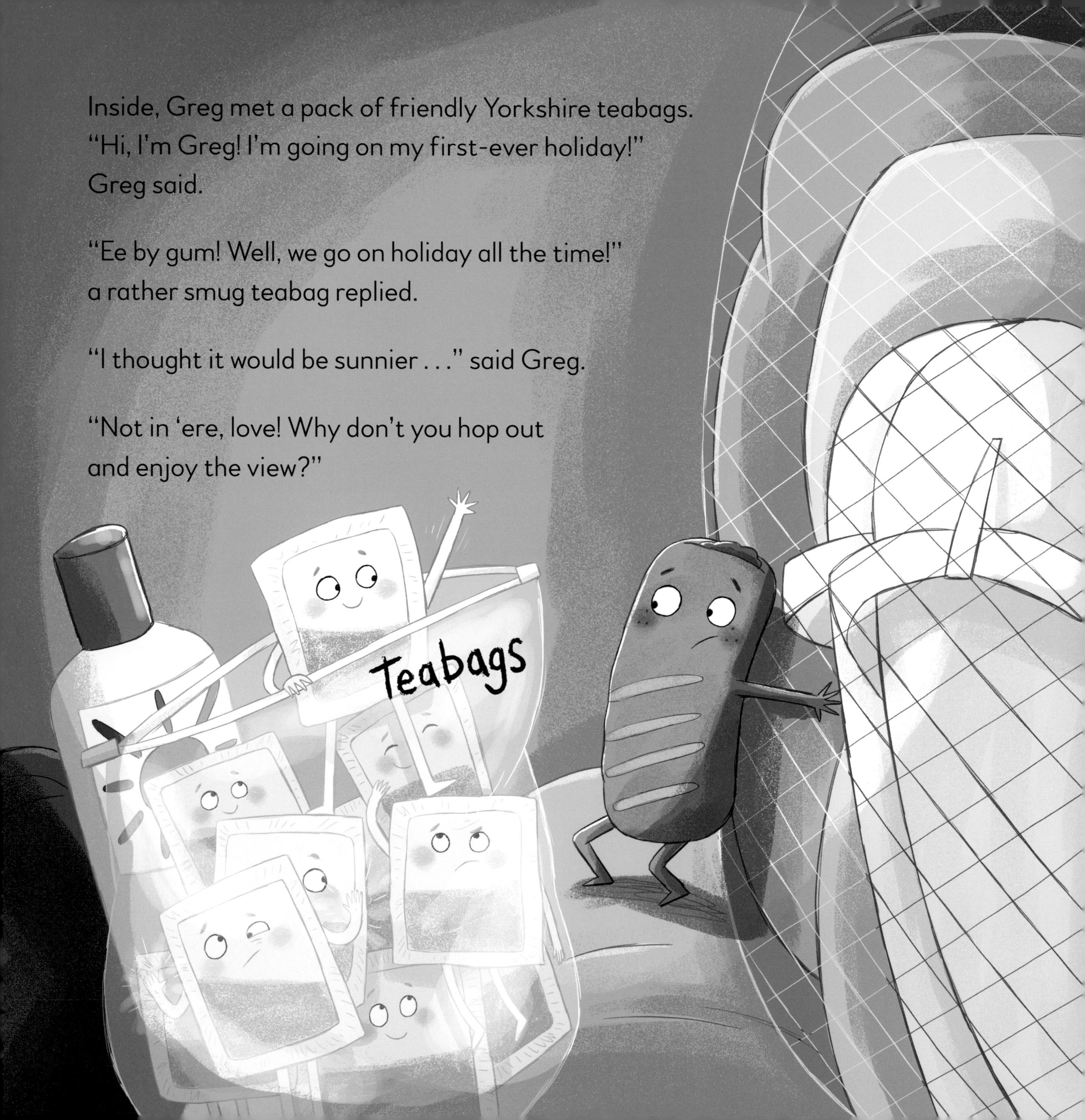

Inside, Greg met a pack of friendly Yorkshire teabags.
"Hi, I'm Greg! I'm going on my first-ever holiday!"
Greg said.

"Ee by gum! Well, we go on holiday all the time!"
a rather smug teabag replied.

"I thought it would be sunnier . . ." said Greg.

"Not in 'ere, love! Why don't you hop out
and enjoy the view?"

Greg grinned from ear-to-ear as he took in all the amazing new sights and sounds. Travelling in style, he felt like a VIP (Very Important Pastry)!

Finally, he arrived at the hotel. "Now this is PARADISE," Greg squealed as he did a running jump into the pool . . .

. . . before enjoying a different kind of pool in the games room!

Then Greg snuggled down under the stars.

"Holidays are the BEST! I can't wait for tomorrow . . ."

The next morning, Greg spotted signs for crazy golf – he definitely didn't want to miss that!

"I can't wait to tell Gloria about this!" he said to himself.

Greg was just about to make friends with a passing gecko when suddenly a golf ball hurtled into him, sending him flying HIGH . . .

. . . on to the windmill,
where he landed SPLAT
on a sail.

"Oh crumbs!" cried Greg,
as a big gust of wind spun the
windmill faster and faster and faster,
launching him into the air once again!

Greg had landed on the busiest beach in Spain!
WHERE could he be? Can you find him?

Greg had managed to gatecrash a picnic!

"Who have you come on holiday with, Greg?" asked Padron Pepper Andre.

"I'm on my own – and I'm having SO much fun," Greg replied. "Although . . ."

Greg thought about Gloria and Holly and all the mini sausage rolls, and he started to feel a bit sad. "Well, I do really miss my friends," he croaked.

"It's OK, you can hang out with us!" cried Cha-Cha Churro. "It's nearly . . .

. . . KARAOKE TIME!"

A karaoke night was JUST what Greg needed.
He grabbed the microphone and waited for the music to start . . .

"This song's dedicated to my sausage-roll sweetheart, Gloria, and all my friends back home!" he cried.

The next morning, the weather was scorching. Greg could feel his corners burning, so he decided to hot-foot it to the coolest place in the town: the ice-cream parlour!

"I'm going to get Gloria's favourite – strawberry ice cream with rainbow sprinkles!" he said excitedly.

As he stepped inside, a blast of cool air hit him and he gazed around in awe . . .

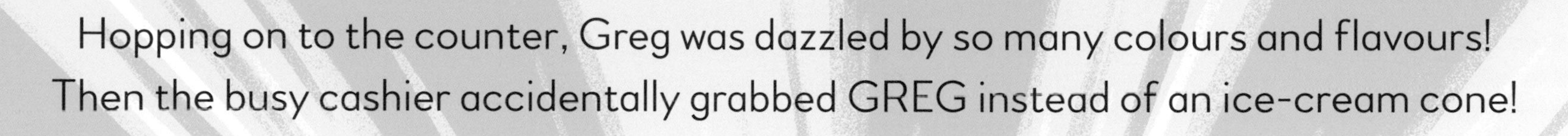

Hopping on to the counter, Greg was dazzled by so many colours and flavours! Then the busy cashier accidentally grabbed GREG instead of an ice-cream cone!

Greg got several scoops of ice cream, a flake, a cherry and lashings of strawberry sauce and sprinkles on his head . . .

before being handed to a delighted little girl, who wandered outside.

But before she could take a bite, a seagull SWOOPED down and snatched Greg straight out of her hand!

Higher and

higher and

higher Greg went, soaring into the sky!

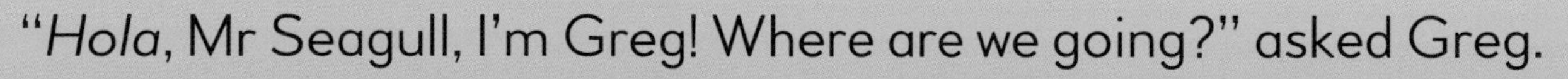

"*Hola*, Mr Seagull, I'm Greg! Where are we going?" asked Greg.
"Oh! Where would you like to go?" replied the confused seagull.
"Well, I'm actually from Britain, and I've got a plane to catch!"

"OK, I can help with that –

HOLD ON TIGHT!"

Greg clung on to Mr Seagull –
he was so excited to be heading
home to see his friends!

MUM, LOOK!
MUSTN'T. LOOK. DOWN!
WE DID IT!

Hasta la vista, pastry!
THANK YOUUUU– *MUCHAS GRACIAAAASSS!*

HOME SWEET HOME. PHEW!
DOUGHNUTS

Back at the bakery, everyone was THRILLED to welcome Greg home.
He couldn't wait to share all his holiday stories, but first . . .
POOL PARTY!

"You know what, Gloria?" said Greg. "I loved my holiday, but I missed you all loads!"
Gloria grinned. "There's no place like home, is there, Greg?"